This Boxer Books paperback belongs to

. . . .

www.boxerbooks.com

For Alfie James Yarrow, born 27th June 2008.
With love, C.M. xxx

First published in hardback in Great Britain in 2009 by Boxer Books Limited.
First published in paperback in Great Britain in 2011 by Boxer Books Limited.
www.boxerbooks.com

Text and illustrations copyright © 2009 Cathy MacLennan
Spooky Doo font copyright © 2009 Cathy MacLennan

A CIP catalogue record for this book
is available from the British Library upon request.

The illustrations were prepared using acrylic paints on blue kraft paper.
The text is set in Spooky Doo.

ISBN 978-1-907152-51-1

1 3 5 7 9 10 8 6 4 2

Printed in China

All of our papers are sourced from managed forests and renewable resources.

Spooky Spooky Spooky!

Cathy MacLennan

Boxer Books

Velvety,
velvety
bats . . .

And horrible howling cats.

Webby webs

and spider
eggs . . .

Then lots and lots and lots of legs.

Spooky spooky spooky!

Rotten rats and bug-eyed flies, gobbling up the pumpkin pies.

Meander, meander,
slip slimy snails,

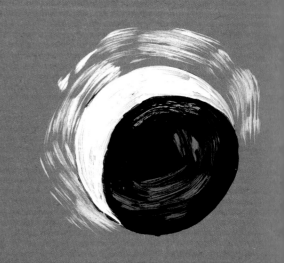

slithery slugs and silver trails.
Spooky spooky spooky!

Plants that climb
and plants that curl,
Wings that swoosh
and eyes that swirl.

The moon, the moon!
What's happened
to the moon?
It's dark,
it's dark,
it's very,
very dark!

On come the lights

of the fireflies . . .

Then bright toothy smiles

and light-up eyes.

Out come the trick-or-treaters to play!

AWAY go
bats and cats,
spiders and rats,
owls and bugs,
snails and slugs.

HOORAY HOORAY HOORAY!

Other Boxer Books paperbacks

Call Me Gorgeous! • **Giles Milton & Alexandra Milton**

Discover a mysterious and fabulous creature in this beautiful book from Giles and Alexandra Milton. It has a porcupine's spines and a crocodile's teeth, a chameleon's tail and a cockerel's feet. What on earth could it be?

ISBN 978-1-907152-49-8

Full Moon Soup • **Alastair Graham**

The full moon seems to be having a strange effect on the guests at the Hotel Splendide. This incredibly detailed book serves up enough spooky goings-on to keep any, young reader occupied for hours!

ISBN 978-1-905417-67-4

I'm Not Scared! • **Jonathan Allen**

Baby Owl is out for a moonlight stroll through the woods, but each animal he bumps into tells him not to be scared! Can Baby Owl convince them that owls are supposed to be out at night and more importantly, that he is not scared?

ISBN 978-1-905417-28-5

www.boxerbooks.com